CW00613656

PRAISE FOR M.

Tom Clancy fans open to a strong female lead will clamor for more.

— *DRONE*, PUBLISHERS WEEKLY

Superb! Miranda is utterly compelling!

— *BOOKLIST,* STARRED REVIEW

Miranda Chase continues to astound and charm.

— BARB M.

Escape Rating: A. Five Stars! OMG just start with *Drone* and be prepared for a fantastic binge-read!

— READING REALITY

The best military thriller I've read in a very long time. Love the female characters.

— *DRONE,* SHELDON MCARTHUR, FOUNDER OF THE MYSTERY BOOKSTORE, LA

A fabulous soaring thriller.

— *Take Over at Midnight,* Midwest Book
Review

Meticulously researched, hard-hitting, and suspenseful.

— *Pure Heat,* Publishers Weekly, starred
review

Expert technical details abound, as do realistic military missions with superb imagery that will have readers feeling as if they are right there in the midst and on the edges of their seats.

— *Light Up the Night,* RT Reviews, 4 1/2
stars

Buchman has catapulted his way to the top tier of my favorite authors.

— Fresh Fiction

Nonstop action that will keep readers on the edge of their seats.

— *Take Over at Midnight,* Library Journal

M L. Buchman's ability to keep the reader right in the middle of the action is amazing.

— LONG AND SHORT REVIEWS

The only thing you'll ask yourself is, "When does the next one come out?"

— *WAIT UNTIL MIDNIGHT,* RT REVIEWS, 4 STARS

The first...of (a) stellar, long-running (military) romantic suspense series.

— *THE NIGHT IS MINE,* BOOKLIST, "THE 20 BEST ROMANTIC SUSPENSE NOVELS: MODERN MASTERPIECES"

I knew the books would be good, but I didn't realize how good.

— NIGHT STALKERS SERIES, KIRKUS REVIEWS

Buchman mixes adrenalin-spiking battles and brusque military jargon with a sensitive approach.

— PUBLISHERS WEEKLY

13 times "Top Pick of the Month"

— Night Owl Reviews

ICE SHELF RESCUE

AN ANTARCTIC ICE FLIERS ROMANCE STORY

M. L. BUCHMAN

Buchman Bookworks

SIGN UP FOR M. L. BUCHMAN'S NEWSLETTER TODAY

and receive:
Release News
Free Short Stories
a Free Book

Get your free book today. Do it now.
free-book.mlbuchman.com

Other works by M. L. Buchman:

Contemporary Romance (cont)

Love Abroad
Heart of the Cotswolds: England
Path of Love: Cinque Terre, Italy

Where Dreams
Where Dreams are Born
Where Dreams Reside
Where Dreams Are of Christmas*
Where Dreams Unfold
Where Dreams Are Written

Science Fiction / Fantasy

Deities Anonymous
Cookbook from Hell: Reheated
Saviors 101

Single Titles
The Nara Reaction
Monk's Maze
the Me and Elsie Chronicles

Non-Fiction

Strategies for Success
Managing Your Inner Artist/Writer
Estate Planning for Authors*
Character Voice
Narrate and Record Your Own
Audiobook*

Short Story Series by M. L. Buchman:

Romantic Suspense

Delta Force
Th Delta Force Shooters
The Delta Force Warriors

Firehawks
The Firehawks Lookouts
The Firehawks Hotshots
The Firebirds

The Night Stalkers
The Night Stalkers 5D Stories
The Night Stalkers 5E Stories
The Night Stalkers CSAR
The Night Stalkers Wedding Stories

US Coast Guard

White House Protection Force

Contemporary Romance

Eagle Cove

Henderson's Ranch*

Where Dreams

Action-Adventure Thrillers

Dead Chef

Miranda Chase Origin Stories

Science Fiction / Fantasy

Deities Anonymous

Other
The Future Night Stalkers
Single Titles

ABOUT THIS TITLE

*Alaskan **bush** **pilot** **Aurora** **Evans** and her trusty Twin Otter cargo plane Myrtle finally found the perfect fit —Antarctica.*

*Glaciologist **Tommy** **Dale** has discovered his life's purpose on The Ice—as locals refer to the continent— facing down climate change one-on-one.*

But when an accident far out on the Larsen Ice Shelf forces a rescue in the heart of a midwinter whiteout, Aurora and Tommy discover a whole new passion.

If they can just survive.

1

"Whoever said scientists were smart, lied!" Aurora Evans glared through Myrtle's windscreen at the white landscape that appeared to spread in every direction—including up.

"Oh I don't know about that, my dear." Doc Tenniel was riding copilot for this flight.

Aurora was too used to flying alone and having only Myrtle to speak with. She and the old de Havilland DHC-6 Twin Otter airplane had been together for a long time. They were each other's constant, and typically only, companions. They could haul nineteen passengers or two tons of cargo just about anywhere. Wheels or pontoons in the summer, but mostly skis down here in Antarctica.

"We scientists have led explorations into every corner of the earth, ocean, and sky. We're quite adept at what we do." He sounded almost...miffed! Which fit, being so British.

She managed not to laugh in his face.

Most "beakers"—Antarctic slang for scientists of any breed, shape, or specialty—wouldn't survive ten minutes without the support crew they never seemed to acknowledge.

"Yet here we are," she nodded toward the non-view, "flying into the vast nothingness on the shortest day of the winter to save a pair of beakers with less sense than God gave a snail."

"A snail is actually a quite sensible creature. First, it eats its own shell to gather calcium and other essential minerals. Then it is able to continuously extrude his or her shell as it grows, and..."

Aurora tuned him out and looked out at all the white.

Someday she'd learn to keep her mouth shut around beakers. Like most men on The Ice, as Antarctica was known to its residents, Doc seemed incredibly pleased to talk to a woman, any woman, even if she wasn't listening.

Scientists might now be thirty percent women on The Ice, but as support personnel they were still few and far between. Gender rarity had its advantages... and someday she'd think of one. In the summer, it was typically easy to find a big enough clump of women to keep the men at bay, but this was her first winter on

The Ice and the slim staff count made it much harder to hide.

Nothing but white ahead, behind, or sideways!

She and Myrtle had been rousted an hour before the Antarctic dawn for a rescue mission. It was actually a misnomer, because there wasn't any dawn during the winter solstice, not at the Brit's Rothera Research Station. This far south on the Antarctic Peninsula, there was a lame twilight for about five hours but that was all she wrote.

She was supposed to be flying back up to Palmer Station today. Located two hundred miles north—clear on the other side of the Antarctic Circle—the US station boasted three hours and forty-four minutes of actual daylight on June 21st.

Except now she wasn't going to be there to see it.

Shortest day of the year but she wasn't going to get a day at all. They'd better get this guy rescued fast, she didn't want to miss the Solstice Night party, too. Even with just ten people of Palmer's summertime forty-five staff wintering over, it was supposed to be a serious amount of fun.

The rescue report stated that a two-man science team was marooned far out on the ice, one critically injured, and nothing else useful. Something going wrong out in the middle of nowhere in midwinter? The only surprising thing was that they weren't *both* dead.

No matter how bad the emergency, rushing things in Antarctica was a fast way to die. Myrtle had the full cold-weather kit, but Aurora had still spent an hour with gas heaters to warm the engines before taking the risk of turning them over. Even a turboprop didn't start well when it was that cold. And replacing an engine was a real strain down here. In winter, it probably couldn't happen at all because the person to fly in the replacement engine...would be herself.

Doc was running down on his evolutionary pathways of personal housing construction methodologies of gastropods.

She offered him a friendly, "Really?"

That seemed to cheer him up and get him rolling again so that she didn't have to interact.

He wasn't only a medico, but also *just so thrilled* by the science of Antarctica that it made her want to dump him from a great height. Scientists could be a major pain, even if carting beakers about was half of her bread and butter. The other half was shuffling around supplies that kept them alive in the first place.

Totally white!

The only thing to see in any direction were Myrtle's nose and wings.

Aurora knew she was safe. Myrtle's instruments insisted they were in straight-and-level flight at five thousand feet up. They were a hundred kilometers south of Slessor Peak, which rose to almost eight thousand feet. The rest of this section of the Antarctandes Range up the middle of the Antarctic Peninsula were under four thousand.

Aside from their altitude, she had to completely trust Myrtle about the flight *attitude*. Though they'd been together long enough for her to trust the old plane's opinion on that.

The instruments don't lie.

It was the very first lesson any pilot learned. She'd been flying long enough to know that actually, on very rare occasions, they did. But it was always for a reason, none of which were relevant at the moment. Myrtle was a trustworthy beast. Aurora leaned forward and patted the console directly below Myrtle's compass.

"Good girl," she whispered too quietly to disturb Doc's ramblings. It didn't matter, Myrtle heard her just fine.

After a decade of bush flying in Alaska, first with Mom, then on her own—after Mom had found a new husband and gone Lower 48—Aurora and Myrtle had landed the golden ticket. For five years (so far), they'd been cruising up and down the Antarctic Peninsula for fun and profit with few problems. Mom's native Alaskan blood had adapted to the heat of Coronado Beach in San Diego overnight. Despite her mixed blood, Aurora still felt like she was dying when the temperature crossed seventy.

Antarctica never came close. A record hot summer

day, high on the Peninsula might approach sixty, but it didn't have the temerity to cross over. And South Pole Station had still never cracked ten degrees. Fine with her.

This year she'd finally landed the lucrative over-winter slot. That ended the last of the quibbles; she was now officially an OAE—Old Antarctic Explorer. Some aspirational geeks said multiple summers counted. But she was with the purists, and a winterover —a single word to a Southie—was required to properly claim the title of OAE.

It was the solstice today, so no matter what happened now, she was in.

Of course, it was only June twenty-first and already a scientist was in trouble out on the ice—the first day of the new Antarctic Year in a very real way. If saving his hide made her miss tonight's solstice party at Palmer, she was going to be rather ticked.

Rather ticked? She'd been spending too much time with the Brits like Doc Tenniel. Majorly bummed! That was better. Pissed off? Yeah!

On the bright side, other than the sun beginning its return, search-and-rescue paid double.

But the white!

Ten miles after she'd taken off from Rothera, she'd torqued the plane enough to look behind her. Yes, she'd still been able to see the spread of buildings, so visibility distance wasn't the issue.

Everything *else* was!

It was all entirely white.

That was a major problem.

She was aloft with no sign of the ground, the sky, or a visible horizon between them.

Aurora listened to the roar of Myrtle's twin Pratt & Whitney PT6A engines. Firm and steady. Even if she wasn't feeling so sure, Myrtle didn't seem to have any doubts which was enough for her.

Myrtle's artificial horizon said she was dead on the mark, the blue half of the instrument floating evenly above the little airplane drawn on the glass with the black half below. With no external visual reference, a pilot could easily fall for a "gut feel" or an inner ear imbalance and end up flying completely upside down without realizing it. When there was no external reference, a body looked inside to find one—and it was always wrong.

The situation reminded her all too clearly about the 1979 tourist plane crash on the other side of the continent. Mt. Erebus was a twelve-thousand-foot peak sticking up out of the flat sea, and the DC-10 airline full of sightseers had run into it head-on, without ever spotting it in a sector whiteout. Two hundred and fifty-seven people, and a DC-10 airliner, all dead.

And she was in the same conditions right now.

The long flat plain of white that was the Larsen Ice Shelf afloat on the Southern Ocean didn't look any different from the ice-clad mountains that formed the backbone of Graham Land, the northern half of the Antarctic Peninsula. By mid-summer, enough of the rocky slopes would have melted out to show the peaks as rock and the valleys as ice.

Not so much in June.

The only real marker in the three-sixty of white was a nebulous brighter-half of the Antarctic haze that said the sun had peeked over the horizon for a few hours somewhere vaguely north...ish. Only her altitude extended her view enough for even that fuzzy hint of morning sunshine; it was going to stay twilight down on the ice until the darkness returned in a few hours.

Their position, close along the Antarctic Circle, meant she had less than five hours of twilight to track down and rescue the two stupid beakers in question.

"See anything yet, Doc?" She had heard enough about gastropods for a lifetime, maybe two. It was far too soon to spot a tent at their last reported position, but at least it gave him something to do.

"Uh, no." He shifted more upright in his seat and began studying the endless white below.

Major science wouldn't start arriving on The Ice until October. By Christmas there'd be four thousand folks scattered across the second largest country in the world, except Antarctica wasn't a country. But for the thousand year-rounders, The Ice was a planet all its own.

Then there were the ones crazy enough to go out and do midwinter research. Winter was a time for hunkering down at your base and playing with your data. Of course, if they did that, there wouldn't be any winter gigs for her and Myrtle.

Flights into the interior were close enough to impossible for six months of the year that only major medical emergencies called for them—the last one four years ago.

But sixteen countries maintained thirty-four bases along the Peninsula and on the South Shetland Islands alone, and half of those were year-rounders. Even the ones not on islands might as well have been. Air travel was the primary connection between them, and with a little cooperation, it was enough to keep her and Myrtle in business through the cold months. She was the nomad of the Peninsula, never long at any base yet always welcome.

If she had a home base, as such, it would be the US base at Palmer Station perched on Anvers Island. Nowhere on the Peninsula was much harsher than central Alaska. Palmer Station was within five miles of being as far south of the equator as Fairbanks was north. Even at the coldest, about minus forty Fahrenheit, fuel was still thirty degrees from freezing.

Doc Tenniel had found a new topic, thankfully a little more relevant. He again began effusing happily in his slightly too urbane English accent, wholly unaware of the freakish nature of the flying that was going on.

"You know, the breakup of a section of the ice shelf in midwinter is wholly unprecedented. Now is normally the time when it's jolly well the safest to explore the ice."

"If you're into freezing your asses off." She knew it was a mistake the moment she said it and was able to recite his predictable reply along with him.

"All in the name of science, Captain. All in the name of science." *Pip. Pip. Cheerio.* Like he was a throwback to Victorian England. Maybe Doc had seen too many Gilbert and Sullivan operettas during med school.

"Yet it's happened," she couldn't resist pointing out. "The Larsen shelf broke in winter."

"Yes, indeed, it is a tad bit puzzling." Maybe his retro-accent was just The Ice. Personality quirks were honed and cherished down here. When they became too irritating, they were cheerfully stomped back into place by other denizens of the base, but they generally thrived.

And even she knew that this midwinter breakup was very strange. The Larsen Ice Shelf was one of the climate change hotspots, shedding thousands of square miles at a time in massive bergs. Originally larger than any New England state except Maine by a factor of three, Larsen had shed an area the size of Connecticut and Rhode Island combined in the span of her own lifetime.

And somewhere out in all that twilit white was a scientific team in trouble.

Sure, she had their GPS coordinates, but the terrain was still a great expanse of nothing but white.

2

"Not one of your smoother moves, Chas."

Chas didn't answer. Hadn't answered once since Tommy had rescued him after the collapse. They were now bundled into their survey tent as the wind slammed it harder than the spring rapids on West River through the Green Mountains. He could do with a dose of Vermont green about now.

But he'd been offered a winterover slot by the Old Man of the Ice himself, Dr. Chas Ellsworth. Tommy hadn't expected to ever even *meet* Antarctica's leading glaciologist. To be selected to assist the Brit with a Larsen Ice Shelf winter study was too incredible an opportunity to pass up. Chas knew more about Larsen than everyone else on the planet—combined.

However, midwinter ice sheets weren't supposed to have surprise crevasses. The only miracle was that Chas had survived rather than plunging to his death.

They'd technically been roped up for safety. Luckily, they were strict on the use of the rope even if it was for an entirely different reason. It was easier to help each other through the blown snow drifts atop the ice shelf when they could haul on each other using the rope.

It was as much security blanket as a communications line—until the ice had disappeared beneath Chas' feet.

The Larsen Ice Shelf was divided into seven sections, A through G. Larsen A had shattered in 1995. Larsen B, over ten thousand years old, had fractured in stages over the last twenty years until only a tiny remnant barely twenty kilometers wide remained. Now Larsen C, by far the largest, was breaking up into monstrous bergs. D through G were all tiny by comparison and, for the moment, safely farther south.

Larsen C was still seventeen thousand square miles and a thousand feet thick. It didn't equate that an area twice the size of his home state of Vermont could just —break. Especially not this far back from the edge.

They'd just unmired their "Doo" and their two sleds from yet another swale filled with wind-blown snow. Chas had stepped aside to take a photo of their rig: Ski-Doo snowmobile, the tow-along supplies trailer stacked high with spare fuel cans, and a second equipment trailer for their ice survey gear. All against the backdrop of the most amazing Aurora Australis he'd ever seen. Intertwined green sheets rippling across the sky like a crazy dragon's laundry. Streaks of gold fire flooding the horizon.

With only five hours of twilight, they started and ended their days in the dark. But what a glorious dark it was.

Astride the Doo, Tommy had turned to face his helmet toward Chas just in time to watch him stumble backward and land on his butt. Which would have been laughable, except a second later, he disappeared from view faster than Wiley E. Coyote after running off the edge of a cliff.

Tommy had already stowed his ice axe alongside the Doo's seat. If he hadn't had his hands on the steering grips, he'd have been yanked off the Doo and dragged across the ice.

They'd both be gone.

As it was, he was fairly sure the harness had cracked a couple of his ribs as he'd fought to arrest Chas' fall.

Tommy had secured the line to the Doo and tied himself to second one before belly crawling to the edge. The crevasse wasn't some little gap in the ice with a snow cap that happened to give way when Chas stepped on it.

Chas' fall had unleashed a ripple collapse that had revealed a five- to ten-meter-wide crack that continued out of sight in both directions.

The first time he'd peered over the edge to see if Chas was alive, Tommy had seen the bottomless pit.

His headlamp didn't touch the darkness. The thousand-foot thickness of the ice shelf appeared to have broken all the way down. Somewhere in depths below, the ocean would be rushing to fill the lower eight hundred feet of the new crack in the ice.

It had taken forever, working with the Doo, to haul Chas up to just below the ice shelf's surface. Each time Tommy crawled back to the precipitous edge to check on Chas' upward progress, it was the single bravest thing he'd ever done—harder every time. Thank God no one was around to see how badly he was quaking in his boots.

The thirty-knot wind seemed intent on driving him over the edge himself. Then, when he turned, it resisted his efforts to return to the Doo and goose it forward another ten or fifteen feet before crawling back to check on Chas again. The blown ice particles against his Doo helmet had sounded like a monster hailstorm on a tin roof each time he faced the wind. And scrubbing his ribs across the ice as he crawled hurt like a son-of-a-bitch.

Easing Chas once more over the cliff's edge by hand, all the while wondering if the section under *his own* butt was going to let go, made any earlier fears seem mild.

Just as he'd finally dragged Chas' unresponsive form onto the ice beside him, and lay there trying to catch his own breath, Tommy had realized the worst of it. The Doo had been parked parallel to the vast crevasse when Chas had fallen. How long had they driven close along the weak spot without knowing? Some glaciologists they were. They should *both* be dead.

Another half hour to get the tent up—far away from the crevasse—and wrestle Chas' dead weight into a sleeping bag. Outside, over the sound of thirty knots of wind chill, it had been impossible to tell if he was even alive. In the tent Tommy could see the tiny cloud of mist each time Chas exhaled—all that gave him away. His own fingers were too numb to feel a pulse over their own throbbing.

He'd called in for a rescue, then just lay there on the tent's thin floor, trying to breathe himself—without moving his ribs.

Some ages later, his radio crackled to life, "This is Myrtle and Aurora calling survey team Larsen Nineteen."

It took him a moment to remember that was him... them technically, but now just him.

"This is Nineteen. Come back."

She verified his GPS coordinates. "I'll be on site in twenty. I need a quarter-mile of skiway with no crevasses or hummocks."

"Right." *Shit!*

He should have thought about that when he called for medevac three hours ago. They'd spent two long weeks winding through the mountains of Graham Land and out onto the ice shelf as part of their survey.

Every five miles they'd stopped for ice cores and radar sounding through the ice to map ice thickness and the terrain below. A methodical, unhurried process that had suited him down to his boots.

Now he had twenty minutes to clear a place for the plane to land or it would fly back where it had come from.

"On it!"

He scrabbled into his cold-weather gear and plunged back into Nature's freezer.

While he'd been inside, the morning dark had brightened into a midday mediocre twilight. Just in case, he reached back into the tent, turned on a high-power flashlight, and aimed it up at the ceiling. From the outside, the tent was now an internally lit bright orange beacon.

That would be one end of the skiway.

Hopefully no worse weather would move in quickly. One good katabatic wind blast, dropping visibility to under three meters in a heartbeat, and he'd be a dead man despite the flashlight.

With no one to rope up to, he selected a ski pole and an ice axe.

Planes landed into the wind. So he turned his back on the wind and stabbed the pole into the surface of ice and snow. Solid. Another step, another stab.

With the wind's help pushing him along, he moved quickly enough. Seven hundred steps, his heart nearly stopping with each one, and he made the distance in under ten minutes without disappearing into an ice crack.

Chance, which had been so unkind to Chas, had favored himself. Not so much as a knee-high drift or an ankle-deep hole.

Now he just needed to get back to the tent so that he could run the Doo up and down the runway a few times to make sure it was smooth enough.

Turning into the wind, he was almost bowled over backwards.

Head-on into thirty knots was a hard push. Like an idiot, he hadn't pulled on his full helmet. Instead he just had snow goggles and his parka's hood—which kept acting like a sail to drag his head backwards.

Out of time, he wrapped a scarf over his mouth and broke into a run. Minus forty degrees with minus thirty more from wind chill. Every breath hurt his battered ribs like a rabbit punch. He was gasping equally from the pain, the effort, and the freezing cold.

"Couldn't stay in Vermont, could you, Tommy Dane? Just had to go be a glaciologist in Antarctica, didn't you?" It was old Professor Farnsworth's fault. There hadn't been a permanent glacier in New England since the last Ice Age. Yet Farnsworth had hooked Tommy's imagination freshman year by showing him how to see that the land had been carved by repeated glaciation like an artist slicing into a woodblock for printing. He'd never lost that wonder;

not even now when it was trying to carve him from the landscape—permanently.

Tommy's footprints were long since swept away.

Every now and then he raised his face enough to adjust his course towards the lit tent. It was like looking into the nozzle of a snow machine on Stowe Mountain ski area—ten thousand particles of ice blasted into every exposed surface each second. And the wind didn't just bite, it roared and growled too loud to hear himself think. Which was a good thing right now.

He was running with all the speed of a tree slug.

When he reached the Doo, he nearly collapsed over the seat. Would have, if there was time. Three more minutes.

Taking just enough time to grab his helmet, he could only pray that the ice, which was firm enough to carry his one-eighty, could also support six hundred pounds of snowmobile. Then, however many tons of airplane.

The Doo fired up on the first try which was also a rare blessing. He unhitched the sleds in favor of speed and raced back down the stretch he'd just explored. He'd only have time for a few passes to pack the snow before the plane arrived.

Ruining his day or the fifteen-thousand-dollar machine he'd signed out was a minor consideration compared to wrecking seven million dollars worth of airplane that was pretty much Chas' only chance of survival.

Aurora and Myrtle were almost here.

The Girls.

They had a real reputation on The Ice. Even during his first summer all the way over at McMurdo on the other side of Antarctica, he'd heard stories about them. The stories weren't real clear about which was the pilot and which the plane; they were always mentioned like they were single unit. You wanted someone to watch your ass out on the ice? Apparently, she...they...The Girls were the ones you wanted.

There were plenty of remarks about how pretty a sight they were, usually followed up with a description of the plane slipping into an impossible landing or airdropping a critical load of supplies.

By the sound of the stories, the workhorse Twin Otter cargo plane was a classic "Antarctic Ten"—a great beauty coming to save your ass but so homely that you'd never look at it twice back in the real world. Even when you weren't in trouble, being way out from base made any connection a real gift. In Antarctica it was easy to be hundreds of miles from the nearest camp—a very lonely feeling.

He discounted all the guy-stories about the pilot being even more worth looking at. When women were in such scarce supply as they were down here, they all took on an aura of Hollywood beauty.

At the end of his second run down and back, he

carved a turn around the tent to set up his third run and aimed once more down his impromptu skiway.

Then, with a hard correction, he almost drove into the tent and right over Chas.

An airplane had appeared out of nowhere. By the time they'd both stopped nose-to-nose, those spinning propellors looked real damn big.

It must have come in behind him as he raced back toward the camp, the Doo's screaming engine trying to drown out the wind's basso howl.

He understood the stories now. The Twin Otter had seen a lot of hard miles. There were deep paint scuffs in her flanks where the spinning propellers had sandpapered the fuselage with bits of ice. The white underbelly was scraped up as well and the red top paint was sun-faded.

And it was about the most damn beautiful sight he'd ever seen. Nothing had ever looked so good as that big steel sky beast come to the rescue.

Before he even shut down the Doo, the propellors were easing to a halt. The instant they did, someone clambered out the right-side door carrying a small case.

"Greetings, my good man. Where's Chas? Had a bit of a fall, did he?"

"About twenty meters."

"Oh dear, and where is he now? Ah, in the tent I see. Well done." And he ducked inside.

Tommy had met Doc Tenniel briefly when he first

arrived at Rothera. Chas had dragged him out onto the ice five times in the three months since he'd come over from McMurdo on the other side of the continent. He hardly knew anyone there, but Doc left an unforgettable impression.

When Tommy turned around, he had to look down abruptly. The pilot was most of a head shorter than he was and had stomped up to stand toe-to-toe with him. Encased in a "Big Red" polar parka, snow pants, and boots, there was little to see other than a shadowed face buried deep within the fur-rimmed hood.

"Nice job guiding me in," she shouted over the wind noise.

If that's what she wanted to believe he was doing, he wasn't going to argue. It—

"Well don't just stand there. I can feel my engines getting cold. Let's go. Go! Go! Go!" As if she and her plane truly were one.

He stumbled back under the sheer force of her words and landed once more on the Doo's seat. Chas rarely spoke a decibel louder than needed, even when telling a joke—the epitome of a soft-spoken Brit, thankfully without Doc's amateur passion for Gilbert and Sullivan that he was always singing along the hallways.

Raw life force vibrated off this woman.

"Don't we have to wait for the Doc?"

"Sure, if you want me to leave your equipment strewn about in the middle of the ice shelf—we're aloft the second Doc has the patient ready. If you aren't aboard, I'll be leaving your ass behind just for good measure. Now move!"

He moved.

She was right. Antarctica, even in high summer, was far too dangerous to traverse alone.

In midwinter?

This survey project was over.

Time to get the hell out.

3

"GREAT, MYRTLE. ANOTHER BEAKER DULLARD. JUST what we needed. 'Oh, I'm just going to sit here on the ice until I freeze to death.' Fine, if he wants to, but I won't do that to my little sister."

"Little sister?" The man scoffed as he came up behind her.

Aurora patted the deck. "She's a total sweetheart. Now get your damned snow machine over here."

"It's the 'little' that I'm having trouble with. She's definitely the big sister."

Aurora eyed him for a moment. A beaker with a sense of humor? Or the knee-jerk flirt of any testosterone-poisoned Antarctic male—which included all of them in her estimation—around any Antarctic female.

She hauled the loading ramp out of Myrtle's cargo

bay, hooked it on the deck edge, and rammed the foot down into the snow.

By the tilt of his head, she knew. He didn't have a clue how to do the next maneuver.

"Okay, get your ass up there. Squat just aft of the door; it's going to happen fast. Whatever you do, don't let me fall back out once I'm aboard."

"What are you—" But he stopped when she walked away toward his Doo which he'd been smart enough to leave on idle.

It was a Ski-Doo Skandic SWT with the full twenty-four-inch tread which was sweet. She raced it a hundred feet or so across the snow to check the throttle reactivity until she had a feel for it.

He was inside, hunched in the four-foot-eleven cabin and close enough to the best spot.

The ramp was ten feet long, only inches wider than the spread of the Doo's skis and rested at about thirty degrees. Easing the skis up onto the ramp, she took a deep breath.

The door was less than four feet high and not much wider. The internal cabin was five feet wide.

And the Doo was ten-six long.

This was always a fun load—not—but she wasn't about to trust some beaker to not drive the Doo through the far side of Myrtle's fuselage.

She goosed and nudged until she was fully on the ramp and the nose was almost to the plane.

When he started to reach out, she shook her head.

"Doesn't he get that you weigh over six hundred pounds, boy? Now you be nice to my Myrtle, okay?"

The low thrum of the Rotax 900 engine offered her a soothing answer.

She rose to her feet but remained hunched low with bent knees. If things went sideway, she was set to spring clear. If they didn't, she had to be low to the machine or she'd catch the top of the door opening in the face.

"Ready?" she called out.

Low thrum from the Doo.

Nod from the beaker.

Afraid of what she'd hear, Aurora didn't wait for her own response.

She gave the throttle a short burst of power.

The Rotax roared to life and jolted her forward.

All in flash, she ducked her head to clear the doorway, the skis hit the deck, and she turned them hard toward the front of the cargo bay. The beaker did a fair job of judging the angle to grab the frame and shove hard *without* jamming his fingers into the drive train. The Doo was now parked facing forward on Myrtle's steel deck.

She nudged the throttle in tiny bursts to walk the Doo up close behind the pair of passenger seats she'd left rigged at the head of the cargo bay, then shut it down.

"You're hired. Now take that litter to the Doc," she

pointed up, where it was tied to the ceiling. "Then get your sleds aboard."

He hesitated with the typical thousand questions.

No, she didn't know why Doc was still in the tent, but it sure didn't look good for whoever the patient was.

Yes, the nearest hospital was the hour back to Rothera.

And hell *yes, she'd been doing this long enough to know what she was doing* despite *being merely a woman.*

"Go!" She shouted at him—again.

Thankfully, he went.

She strapped down the Doo so that it couldn't shift on her during flight.

By the time she was done, he had the first of the sleds propped on the ramp. She grabbed the tongue and pulled, watching him as he pushed from behind.

"You're making mighty hard work of that." She eased the first one to the rear.

"Busted a couple of ribs, I think." But he didn't stop with lining up the second sled.

"Why'd you go and do that?" *Weird!* A beaker who didn't just sit on the ice and wait to have his ass rescued because he had a hangnail.

"It was the best way out of a winter survey mission that I could come up with. Tossing Chas into a crevasse seemed like a good idea before I remembered we were roped together."

"Paybacks can be hell."

"Yep. Next time I'll remember to cut the rope first."

They got the second sled in. She felt bad about

making him help heft it on top of the other one, but she couldn't shift it herself. The cargo bay was only eighteen feet long and the first ten of it was now filled with Doo and a narrow passageway forward. They still had to stow an occupied litter and leave room for Doc to work beside it.

"Actually," he knelt to help her strap the sleds in place with only a small groan. "Tossing him in was the only way I could think of to meet the most famous girls on the northern ice."

"Most famous girls on the northern ice? Should I ask for what?" That he included Myrtle was in his favor.

"For being unbelievably awesome. And," he waved a hand toward Myrtle's ceiling, "I've already seen the Aurora Australis, which is beyond gorgeous. I figured I should do a little comparing. One Aurora to another." Then he patted the plane as if he thought she herself was the one named Myrtle.

"And now that you've met both of the Auroras?" She kept her smile aimed away from him.

"Are you kidding? The plane that's fetching our busted-up behinds off the Larsen Ice Shelf in the middle of winter, or some pretty lights in the sky? Zero contest. Though those are some seriously pretty lights. Just saying, so that she knows how high the praise is." He patted Myrtle again.

"If you're trying to get on my plane's good side, you're doing a fine job of it." She finished the last strap.

"How about on *your* good side? Because, damn, I've been riding Doos since I was knee-high to a ski-lift, and I couldn't have done that half as sweet."

"Where you from, Beaker?"

"Vermont." He didn't even hesitate at the nickname.

"Well, that's the problem. You only get to ride a few months of the year. Fairbanks, Alaska we get to ride October to April—on the short years."

That he was flirting was her standard shut-down switch. It wasn't like the stories of harassment or shut-out that were standard in the '70s through the '90s, but the flirt-wave was still pretty unrelenting anywhere she went on The Ice. And typical of most stations, there was only one other woman at Palmer. It helped that she was the Station Chief but there weren't a lot of crowds to fade into, especially with the winter dropping the staff numbers down.

Still, it was nice that he included Myrtle. That earned him a short-term minimum-level flirting license.

4

TOMMY HARDLY KNEW WHAT HE WAS BABBLING ABOUT. He just knew if he stopped before they were airborne, he was done for. His ribs were killing him, but he wasn't coughing up blood, so he'd still go with bruised or cracked over broken.

"Could use a hand here please?" A high-brow British accent addressed him from the cargo bay door.

Doc didn't even lose his affected accent in an Antarctic windstorm over an unconscious patient. Though, to his credit, he'd dragged the litter over by himself.

"How's he doing, Doc?"

"This chap is alive enough to load him aboard a warm plane. We'll get him aloft and then I'll take the time to assess his condition in a touch more detail."

"Fewer words, more action," the pilot called out.

Tommy jumped down to the snow and collapsed

the rest of the way to the ice when his side exploded with pain. It was so bad that his vision tunneled briefly.

"Slipped," he managed to mutter while struggling back to his feet.

The three of them loaded the unresponsive Chas aboard and strapped him in.

A snap in the high wind drew his attention back to the tent. No longer weighted down with Chas's body, it was now struggling hard against the ice screws he'd used in lieu of tent pegs. With the flashlight inside, it still glowed bright orange in the heavy dusk.

He headed over to break it down, but Myrtle the pilot shouted after him. What parent in this age named their kid Myrtle?

"Hey! Leaving now!"

"Get Aurora running. No footprint, remember." Even urine was loaded into bright yellow U-barrels and shipped back out.

If she said anything, it was ripped away by the wind. His few minutes aboard and in the plane's wind shadow had made him forget the abuse the weather was handing out.

The frail dusk was already fading, and the wind was whipping even harder than before. The haze that had moved in earlier assuredly blotted out the Aurora Australis; he didn't waste the time or energy to check.

He didn't bother with any niceties as the first engine coughed to life behind him. He slid free and folded the poles in one fist, pulled the ice screws with the other hand, then threw himself bodily on the fabric as it was tossed downwind.

As if he were some filter-feeding krill using setae like fingers to rake food toward its maw, Tommy scrabbled at the nylon with his fists and feet, bunching it under his body. When the bundle of the tent—with Chas' sleeping bag, and the still-lit flashlight that kept trying to blind him through the thin nylon—and he were about the same size, he struggled to his feet.

The propellors kept beating louder and louder until they drowned out the wind's roar sweeping over the Antarctic ice.

The wind kept catching the bundled-up tent he held in both arms, and continued to drag him back and forth over the ice.

He gave the whirling propellors a wide berth, though once he passed behind the wings, their backdraft nearly blew him beyond the tail. Next stop South Georgia Island thirteen hundred miles downwind.

With the doc's help from above, he managed to shove the tent into the cargo door before it beat him to death.

But there was no way in hell he could lift himself up.

The propellors changed tone and the wind by the cargo door lessened. At least he could stand now without hanging on. Much.

As he clung to the edge of the cargo deck, the pilot came back. She jumped out beside him.

"Come on, we're not done yet."

He was.

But he followed her anyway. She was carrying a two-step-high ladder and two hanks of rope.

At the end of the wing, she climbed the ladder and slipped one rope through a ring loop on the underside.

"Hold this. We're going to take turns trying to rock the plane."

"Why?" He took the doubled-over line. It kept him upright just as well as the edge of the cargo deck.

"Skis froze to the ice and I can't break her loose with just the engines. I'm going to the other wing and —" She tipped her forearm back and forth like a teeter totter. "Don't worry about hurting the wing. She can take a lot more than we can give her."

It was hard to believe that a woman her size could have any effect on such a large object as the DHC-6 Twin Otter. Then he looked at the thirty-foot-long wing, thought about what could be done with a lever arm of that length, and decided that Myrtle was a smart woman. A hundred-pound force with that kind of lever advantage could produce more than a half-ton of lifting force at the frozen skis. His own weight could deliver well over a ton. They had to rotate the plane and its cargo as well, but he wasn't up for that kind of math at the moment.

He bent down far enough to watch her progress under the plane.

Ladder in place.

Her feet disappearing up the ladder.

Two ends of rope dangling down together.

Then her feet appearing suddenly and dangling a foot in air as she jumped off the ladder while hanging onto the rope like a crazed monk in some mythic bell tower.

His rope barely twitched in his hands.

He took a deep breath and threw his weight into the rope in turn.

It hurt, but not as badly as jumping out of the plane.

Nothing.

But as soon as his wingtip tweaked slightly upward showing she'd jumped again; he gave his best counterpull.

They found a rhythm that built naturally.

Still nothing.

Tommy knew he couldn't sustain this much longer.

He lunged up as high as he could and threw his weight against the line.

Something gave.

At first, he thought it was his ribs as his knees hit the ice.

But then he was being hauled upward by the momentum of the rocking wing.

The opposite ski had broken free from the ice.

Despite his not letting go, the counterswing was enough to break free the near-side ski.

The pilot raced around to the open cargo bay doors. She set the ladder by the door and waved for him to hurry.

Right! They needed to get moving before the plane's weight on the skis refroze the ice.

Dragging the rope behind him, he managed to climb the two steps, turn, and sit on the cargo deck. She shoved his feet hard enough to make him tumble back onto Chas, and make the doctor protest with a hearty, "Here now. Have a care."

She tossed the ladder aboard, hopped up as if the cargo deck wasn't nearly shoulder-high on her, then slammed and latched the cargo doors.

In a flash, she was gone forward.

This time, when the engines roared to life, he could feel the plane nosing down slightly as the engines drove ahead on the high wings. Right. The nose ski would still be firmly anchored in the ice.

Then it all broke loose at once and, with one hard jerk, they were on the move. And...up.

In too much pain to do more, he slumped on the deck, so glad to be out of the cold and wind that he could cry and prayed that the pilot was as good as her plane.

5

"Rothera just won't do," Doc Tenniel came forward to fill her in before she'd climbed Myrtle to five thousand feet.

"What do you mean?" Aurora didn't need any more trouble. They'd come so close to being frozen into the ice that she'd been scared literally spitless.

The wind had picked up another ten knots just in the time they'd been loading. If she'd really been frozen in hard, they might not have gotten her aloft again until Antarctica unleashed one of his hundred-mile-an-hour winds. A katabatic blast that would break Myrtle out of the ice and tumble her to pieces.

"This chap," Doc nodded to the rear, "he's rather busted up."

Aurora had to breathe carefully before she could speak. Her first reaction had been that the helpful beaker, whose name she still didn't know, was the one

Doc was referring to. She liked him and didn't like the image of him being worse off than she thought he was. But, of course, Doc would be talking about his patient.

"Dr. Chas Emerson has need of major medical, more than I can provide at Rothera Research Station."

"Where do we have to go?"

"Our choices are Amundsen-Scott—"

"There's no *way* I'm flying to the South Pole in midwinter!" With the waystation refueling camps closed for the winter, it would mean loading up several drums of fuel and taking off thousands of pounds overweight. It would be a massive strain on Myrtle. And the midwinter conditions there were so much harsher than the Peninsula that if she made it there, she might not make it back out—ever.

"The other option is Punta Arenas, over in Chile. The hospital there is sufficient if I can keep him alive that long."

She calced the fuel in her head. It was in range because Myrtle had the extended range fuel tanks and Aurora had made sure that they topped up her fuel at Rothera. In range...barely...depending on the weather.

Aurora reached for the radio to get an update. If they were going to fly over the Drake Passage all the way to the Strait of Magellan, she'd need all the help she could get.

"Patch up Beaker Boy and get him up here."

"Patch him up, you say? What's wrong with him?"

She could feel Doc Tenniel raising his eyebrows in British puzzlement even if she couldn't turn to see it.

"Busted ribs. Get them taped or whatever it is you do. Make sure any painkillers you give him aren't sleepies. I need a hand to do this. Now go!"

Three or four *skilled* hands would be better, but she'd have to work with what she had.

6

"HOLY HELL! YOU CAN'T EXPECT ME TO HELP YOU WITH this, Myrtle." He'd seen cockpits before, at a safe distance. But to actually sit in one of the pilot's seats and...touch things?

"She has low expectations."

"Why do you have low expectations? Not saying it's inaccurate. And do you always talk about yourself in the third person? Just asking."

"Shut up! Sit down! Buckle up!"

At a loss for what else to do, he followed orders and sat in the right-hand seat. Which was easier to do with the heavy tape Doc had laid across his ribs. Then he began trying to figure out the four-point seat belt harness.

"Sorry," she apologized. "This is just a little unnerving at the moment. What's your name? Mine's Aurora, by the way. Myrtle is my plane."

"Oh, I screwed that up some, didn't I? I'm Tommy," then he looked to his left. "Holy hell!"

"What now?" She said it with a sigh.

Myr—*Aurora* wasn't an *Antarctic* Ten. He was sure that he remembered what beautiful women *really* looked like, and they rarely looked this good. She'd shed her Big Red over the back of the seat. A straight fall of jet-black hair reached past her shoulders. Her skin was the brown of fresh earth beneath a shining sun. And a snug turtleneck revealed...more than he should be thinking about right now.

Her second sigh said she knew exactly what he was thinking.

"Well," he did his best to recover, "you're giving me a major concern now."

"Which is?" She was remaining determinedly focused out the windscreen.

"If your plane isn't named Aurora, did I insult her by comparing her to the Aurora Australis?"

She might have smiled, which he'd take as a good sign.

So, he turned back to the dazzling array of dials and gauges that confronted him. There was also a second steering wheel just like the one Aurora was holding.

"Your big sister Myrtle may have looked like heaven slipping down out of the skies, but she's scaring the crap out of me right about now. Glaciologists are interested in extraordinarily little other than ice and the ground it runs over. We're kind of boring that way."

"Okay, so we'll start with icing factors. We're presently flying in air that is minus thirty degrees with a humidity of eighty percent. What does that tell you?"

"Ice formation occurs rapidly. Like the hoary rime that you see on old sailing ships or Chicago lighthouses. You know, that really cool picture of the storm off Lake Michigan coating that whole lighthouse in massive icicles and—"

"And!" she cut him off. "When we get ice on our wings and propellor?"

"Oh." The answer to that didn't require advanced mathematics. Rough and heavy ice, wrapping around wings and disrupting air flow, would decrease lift. Not something he wanted happening to any airplane he was riding in.

"So, Mr. Glaciologist. Care to tell Myrtle and me what we're flying into?" She tapped a small screen that must be a radar. "Along with this?" She peeled a tablet computer he hadn't noticed Velcroed to one of her thighs and handed it over.

He studied the satellite map, managed to orient that image with what he was seeing on the radar screen, and read through the weather data on the tablet. He wasn't used to the format, but you didn't study glaciers, or live in a place like Antarctica, without knowing weather.

"Um, how high can Myrtle fly?"

"Twenty-five thousand feet."

"Get up there. And veer west."

"Veer? I don't have a lot of spare fuel to go veering about the sky. Punta Arenas is a long way off."

He expanded the view to focus on the storm pattern developing over the Southern Ocean.

"If you start out high. The jet stream will carry you east. But there's a storm developing over the Drake Passage. The winds—man, that's so weird, I'm still not used to the fact that Southern storms spin counterclockwise, it just looks wrong. Anyway, once over the Drake Passage between the Antarctic Peninsula and Tierra del Fuego if you drop lower, out of the jet stream, you should be able to ride the curl of developing storm that will sweep you back to the east a bit. Does that work in flying? I don't know, but I think it makes sense."

She looked at him for a long moment. "Who are you?"

"Hi, I'm Tommy." He held out a hand and she shook it, keeping her left hand on the wheel. Strong grip of a woman who worked for a living. "I'm a glaciologist. Think I already mentioned that. It means I'm a bit of a weather nerd."

Her big eyes were almost as dark as her hair and dominated her slender face.

She held his hand for an extra moment, which was genuinely nice. He'd had an early girlfriend teach him the joys of just holding hands.

"Yeah, that works in flying. And thanks. I've never made this crossing in winter, but you just confirmed my flight plan. That storm will be a rough ride, so let's get you up to speed on some of Myrtle's other tricks. Rest your hand lightly on the controls."

Tommy let go of her hand and wrapped it around his steering wheel's right handgrip. He could feel the warmth of Aurora's hand on Myrtle's cold plastic.

When Aurora shifted the wheel, he could feel it move beneath his own hand. It was far more intimate than he'd ever have guessed.

7

Aurora had radioed down to Palmer Station as she passed overhead while Doc Tenniel was still bandaging Tommy's ribs.

It was just as well that he hadn't come forward yet. She'd had a tentative solstice night assignation with Palmer's chief carpenter and fix-it-man. He didn't understand planes, at all, but he was always glad to lend a skilled wrench when she'd needed it. An excuse to "hang with The Girls" was definitely part of it, but he hadn't been pushy which she appreciated.

Not that she'd been particularly looking forward to being someone's ice-wife—because what happened on The Ice stayed on The Ice. But the winters were long and cold, and some companionship would be nice.

Of course, he'd been the one to answer her call to Palmer about her missing the solstice.

He joshed her some about jumping ship the first

night of being an OAE, but after five years she'd earned the Old Antarctic Explorer fair and square and it was only friendly teasing. He was dealt with quickly and with little regret, at least on her side.

It was Tommy, after his first flying lesson, who made sure she ate. He'd raided the container where she kept a couple weeks of emergency supplies—because you didn't fly over the ice with less. His own supplies were tied down inside the two sleds.

He somehow made energy bars and near-frozen dried fruit into a droll celebration.

A lunch of a mac and cheese MRE—Meal Ready to Eat—was a pleasant surprise. She forgot she'd stocked those.

She hadn't flown with anyone since Mom had quit and gone south leaving her the old cargo plane. It was...nice. Half of it was a second set of eyes on the instruments, and half just moral support.

Especially when the flying turned hard.

Larsen Ice Shelf to Punta Arenas was only a five-hour flight—which would give her a fuel reserve of half an hour, if nothing went wrong. And it was four-and-a-half hours from landfall to landfall.

Once well clear of the shore, their descent below the east-racing jet stream, which moved at fully half the speed of her plane—over a hundred miles an hour —plunged them down into a rugged storm. Doc Tenniel wasn't happy about her battering his patient, but she wasn't happy about the flying battering Myrtle, so they were even. The advantage was that it was fast, saving her the fuel for when she hit the hard headwind over Tierra del Fuego.

Definitely not an autopilot route, this kind of flying was hard work and there was never a single second's break. She just had to gut it out.

After crossing the harsh mountains of Tierra del Fuego, they finally hit the Strait of Magellan and she could cruise low over the glassy water. Her clenched shoulders began to unwind like slipping into a hot bath—another luxury that didn't happen on The Ice. Fresh water was scarce, collecting and melting snow took a lot of energy, both human and heaters, and showers were regulated to under two minutes.

The descent into Punta Arenas was...startling. A town of a hundred thousand—a hundred times the winter population of the entire continent she'd just left —it lay on the north shore of the narrow Strait of Magellan. The buildings were perched along the water like bright orange, blue, and pink birds who'd arrived during migration then forgotten to move on.

Even though it was winter, and everything was coated in a layer of white snow, there were windswept places revealing brown grasses and occasional trees offering flashes of green. But this was the first natural color other than rock, dirt, ice, or ocean since she'd last gone south last October.

She knew that "greenout" was supposed to be as dramatic as a whiteout—people had told her about not being able to look at anything else when first seeing green. But this was the first time she'd experienced it for herself. Even though the flecks of color were so few and far between, they still distracted her so badly she was amazed that she executed the landing at all.

Doc Tenniel had called ahead and had an ambulance waiting. He took Tommy's number and promised to call the moment there was news.

Within three minutes of landing after the brutally taxing flight, there was just...silence.

No engine roar. No creaking of Myrtle's wings as she slammed through pockets of turbulence like the trooper she was. No more staring at the fast-descending fuel gauge every thirty seconds and rerunning the math of remaining flight time versus fuel flow.

Suddenly it was just her and Tommy, standing on the tarmac. She locked up Myrtle, arranged for refueling, and stood out in the warmth of the setting sun.

"Good job," Tommy grinned, then turned to pat Myrtle's nose. "Oh. You, too," he added to Aurora herself as an offhand afterthought that made her laugh just as he'd intended.

It was two degrees above freezing, sixty-five degrees warmer than the Larsen Ice Shelf, and the wind was a mild five to ten knots. They both stood in light jackets as the ground crew in full parkas and heavy gloves hurried to get the refueling done as fast as possible so that they could retreat back to their warm hidey hole.

She waited only long enough to make sure they were loading AN-8 fuel instead of JP-8 fuel. ANtarctic-8 or Ice-8, as it was sometimes called, froze fourteen degrees lower than standard jet propellant fuel.

"What now?" Seven hours of hard flying had taken it out of her, she could barely stand.

"Do you know Punta Arenas?"

"I've never been past the airport. I fly through here each season for fuel, but that's about it. Southbound I'm eager to get on The Ice and northbound I can't wait to get away."

"Yep!" Tommy agreed. "Sounds about right. I got laid-over here for a week once."

"Are there a week's worth of things to do here?"

"You've got to be kidding me!" She was getting very used to Tommy's laugh. "But I learned some things. Are you a nice sit-down meal kind of woman or—"

"Burger and a beer."

"How about freshies?"

"Oh my god! Actual vegetables?"

"First Caesar salad north of The Ice." Tommy signed out one of the rental cars reserved for pilots.

"That does it, I'm yours!" Aurora couldn't quite believe the words that came out of her mouth but, rather to her surprise, she didn't have a lot of interest in taking them back.

Not as they split a monster salad.

Not as they shared his pizza and her burger.

Not as they tumbled into bed together in a local hotel.

And both crashed into sleep harder than a plane landing with no wings.

8

"I've been robbed!" Tommy groaned when he woke up alone in the morning.

His ringing phone had rousted him, and no beautiful pilot lay beside him.

"What?" he snapped at the caller. Then he spotted Aurora's gear bag still dumped on a chair and felt a little better.

"Good morning to you, too." Doc Tenniel sounded typically bright and chipper despite—Tommy checked his watch—it being only six a.m. "Do you always begin your days being surly?"

"Yes!" Tommy rubbed at his face, then became aware of the shower running. That put a much brighter spin on the morning. "It's in the top secret *How to Be an American* handbook."

"Ah, as I always suspected. Well, you'll be glad to know that Dr. Emerson made it through the surgery. A few more hours and we might have had some rather critical issues, but we were able to tie off the bleeder in his head before it damaged his brain. His full recovery looks very hopeful. I told him you were still local, and he is anticipating a visit."

"Uh…" A vision strolled out of the bathroom in a robe that was tied at the waist but was revealing enough cleavage and leg to kill a man.

"Mr. Dane?"

"Uh…huh?"

Aurora strolled over, still rubbing her hair in a towel. She leaned over the bed, offering him an amazing view down the front of the robe, then sniffed loudly before pinching her nose. "Far doo longa on da ice."

Then she slipped the phone from his nerveless fingers. "Hi Doc? Yes, I'm sorry. Tommy is just a beaker, so we can't expect much from him. He's looking a little toasty at the moment—perhaps I should bring him by the hospital for testing."

"Toasty" was an Ice epithet for the brain fog and forgetfulness caused by the dark, cold, and high altitude of much of Antarctica.

He'd show her he wasn't toasty.

She sidestepped his attempt to grab her, then pointed imperiously toward the bathroom, before pinching her nose again.

"Really? That's wonderful news," she continued her conversation with Doc.

Tommy didn't wait around to find out what was wonderful. The faster he showered, the sooner...well... yeah. That was his idea of wonderful at the moment.

Competent women were a major turn-on for any rational-thinking man. And being a "beaker" he considered himself to be very rational.

Aurora hadn't only proven herself competent on the ice and in the air. She'd also been one of the best dinner companions he'd ever had. Bright, funny, and took her adventures head-on. Maybe it was the Alaskan bush pilot in her. Maybe it was the joy of the Antarctic that seemed to strike so few but created a community within the community. The bottom of the world had definitely snared her as thoroughly as it had snared him.

And now he was looking forward to a whole new kind of wonderful.

Except by the time he was out of the shower, she was dressed and leaning against the doorframe watching him.

"Why..."

She handed him back his phone as he stood there naked, dripping on the tile floor. He knew they were headed to the hospital.

"Couldn't Chas have the decency to stay out of it for another few hours like any other decent man?"

"No, but they are medevacing him out on the next flight. So visiting him at the hospital is now or never."

"Shit!"

"Too bad you're all wet or I'd jump you right now, Beaker Boy."

He hurried to dry himself, but she was already in boots and parka by the time he was done. All he had with him were heavy field clothes, but he had one set that wasn't too ripe yet.

9

"WHAT IN THE WORLD HAPPENED?"

Tommy pulled up the new satellite radar image he'd grabbed onto his tablet during the drive over. He turned it for Chas to see.

"You personally created a brand-new iceberg with your butt—about the only thing you didn't break." He did his best not to look at the bandages swaddling Chas' head or the casts on his arm and leg. Life was not supposed to be so fragile. "Depending on how the crack runs, it could be bigger than A-68."

Chas opened his eyes wider then narrowed them... then sighed in frustration. "I can't focus on the screen. I won't remember any of this when the drugs wear off. Send me everything you can so that I can review it when I'm not high on whatever this stuff is. Not complaining. I happily can't feel a thing, but I barely remember you arriving five minutes ago."

"I've been here for hours."

Chas barked a laugh. "I could almost believe you. How did I get to Punta Arenas, anyway?"

Tommy offered a very abbreviated version of his rescue. "Doc Tenniel flew in from Rothera and he insisted on getting you to a real hospital immediately. We flew here direct from Larsen."

Chas was nodding at the ceiling. "Was it The Girls?"

Before Tommy could answer, Chas continued.

"Hell of a pair. You should track them down. Serious pair of lookers."

Tommy cleared his throat and glanced over at Aurora leaning against the wall on the opposite side of the bed. She was grinning at him.

Chas' eyes were drifting shut. "Though she's too smart for you."

"Who's too smart for me, Myrtle the plane?"

"Definitely, but the woman half of that team is even smarter."

"Say what? I've got a PhD from Dartmouth and..."

"Nope. She doesn't stoop to doing it with mere ice men." He raised a hand, dragged along an IV line, a blood pressure cuff, an oxygen meter, and finally tapped his temple knowingly. He added something that might have been a wink or might have been a grimace when he noticed all the gear still attached to him.

Aurora shrugged a "Maybe yes."

He liked that she stayed above the ice-wife/ice-husband shuffling that always seemed to be going on down there. It made sharing a bed with her, even while passed out, and a shower, even separately, all the more special.

"You can admire. But don't try to touch. Shove you...right out of that...plane of hers. At altitude." Chas' voice, which had been fading, snapped back and he reopened his eyes. "Hey!"

"Yes, Chas?"

"When did you get here, Tommy?"

"Hours ago, Chas. Never left your side."

Aurora's snort of laughter didn't draw Chas' attention to his other side.

"Good man. Good man." His eyes were closing again. "You're Head of Ice at Rothera now. Take over for me. Needs someone like you. Smart."

"As smart as The Girls?"

"Nope. Not as good looking either. You'll meet them someday, but don't even waste your time dreaming. I'm old enough to be her father, but you're still a young whipper snapper and probably think that means something. She'll knock that out of you soon enough. Watched her do it to enough other young bucks." Chas closed his eyes again. "You take care of my ice. Time I went back...to the...real...world." This time he went fully to sleep, proven by his heart monitor's slower beeps.

Head of Ice? Had Emerson really meant that?

It wouldn't be nearly that straightforward but... He'd wait to see what Emerson said when he was better, and off the drugs.

Still, the idea didn't just melt away. Chief glaciologist at Rothera Research Station was a height that no one climbed because the fixture of Dr. Chas Emerson was always in place.

After the two summers he'd spent at McMurdo and the Pole, Chas had requested him by name to be the only other glaciologist to do a winterover on the Peninsula. There were still a couple at McMurdo and two more at the Pole, but they all fed their data through Chas.

Duh! He slapped his forehead. The data flow that Chas had him handling for the last three months. Chas *had* been grooming him to take over.

Which meant his drugged-out offer was probably serious.

"Full time on The Ice?"

"That's what he said," Aurora spoke for the first time. She wasn't smiling or frowning. She was... looking thoughtful.

"You thinking of being down there full-time for a while?"

She watched him with those big dark eyes as seriously as when he'd interpreted the weather patterns with her.

That's when he figured out what he'd just sort of asked.

Aurora started to smile as the light dawned.

He'd just asked her if she'd be staying somewhere they could be together. They hadn't done more than share a flight, a meal, and a bed—for sleeping. But the question was still real.

During the flight and over dinner, they discovered a shared love of Antarctica. They were both sufficiently renegade to fit in on The Ice.

Maybe they'd start as ice-wife and ice-husband, but Chas had said she was too smart for that.

Well, maybe he could be smart, too. Because it was sure easy to imagine someday finding someone to fill his shoes just as Chas had found him. Then the two of them—three with Myrtle—could fly off on yet another new adventure together.

Maybe he *was* smart enough to do that.

Her smile said that she already was.

He slipped lower in his chair and propped a foot on Chas' hospital bed.

She raised her eyebrows in question.

"You know," he tried his best to sound as if he was discussing the next spot to drill an ice core. "We kind of fell asleep before we had a chance to celebrate the solstice."

"We did."

At her continued smile, he kept his silence and raised his own eyebrows in question.

"Well," she shrugged as if it had no consequence, "that storm in the Drake Passage is going to take another day to blow out. We could celebrate the New Year a day late. If its important to you."

There was the key word. To be with a woman like Aurora, it had to be important, not casual.

Did he want that? Did he *feel* that? After a single day from twilight on the ice to the sunrise now shining in the hospital window? After a life of only "casual," he now knew that "important" felt completely different.

"Not really the solstice anymore," he nodded toward the light sparkling off the melting snow outside.

"Not really," she agreed. "It's more the first day of *The Ice's* new year." She emphasized it just enough to make it clear The Ice was home, at least for now. He liked the sound of that—a lot.

"Instead of celebrating the solstice, we could celebrate the First Night. The First Night of..." But he was smart enough not to say the next thought aloud.

Her nod and smile acknowledged the thought.

There was no need for words.

Their future began today.

DRONE (EXCERPT)

IF YOU ENJOYED THAT, YOU'LL LOVE
MIRANDA CHASE!

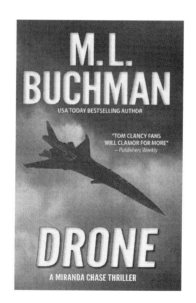

DRONE (EXCERPT)

Flight 630 at 37,000 feet
12 nautical miles north of
Santa Fe, New Mexico, USA

THE FLIGHT ATTENDANT STEPPED UP TO HER SEAT—4E—
which had never been her favorite on a 767-300. At
least the cabin setup was in the familiar 261-seat, 2-
class configuration, currently running at a seventy-
three percent load capacity with a standard crew of ten
and one ride-along FAA inspector in the cockpit jump
seat.

"Excuse me, are you Miranda Chase?"

She nodded.

The attendant made a face that she couldn't
interpret.

A frown? Did that indicate anger?

He turned away before she could consider the possibilities and, without another word, returned to his station at the front of the cabin.

Miranda once again straightened the emergency exit plan that the flight's vibrations kept shifting askew in its pocket.

This flight from yesterday's meeting at LAX to today's DC lunch meeting at the National Transportation Safety Board's headquarters departed so early that she'd decided to spend the night in the airline's executive lounge working on various aviation accident reports. She never slept on a flight and would have to catch up on her sleep tonight.

Miranda felt the shift as the plane turned into a modest five-degree bank to the left. The bright rays of dawn over the New Mexico desert shifted from the left-hand windows to the right side.

At due north, she heard the Rolls-Royce RB211 engines (quite a pleasant high tone compared to the Pratt & Whitney PW4000 that she always found unnerving) ease off ever so slightly, signaling a slow descent. The pilot was transitioning from an eastbound course that would be flown at an odd number of thousands of feet to a westbound one that must be flown at an even number.

The flight attendant then picked up the intercom phone and a loud squawk sounded through the cabin. Most people would be asleep and there were soft complaints and rustling down the length of the aircraft.

"We regret to inform you that there is an emergency on the ground. I repeat, there is nothing wrong with the plane. We are being routed back to Las Vegas, where we will disembark one passenger, refuel, and then continue our flight to DC. Our apologies for the inconvenience."

There were now shouts of complaint all up and down the aisle.

The flight attendant was staring straight at her as he slammed the intercom back into its cradle with significantly greater force than was required to seat it properly.

Oh. It was her they would be disembarking. That meant there was a crash in need of an NTSB investigator—a major one if they were flying back an hour in the wrong direction.

Thankfully, she always had her site kit with her.

For some reason, her seatmate was muttering something foul. Miranda ignored it and began to prepare herself.

Only the crash mattered.

She straightened the exit plan once more. It had shifted the other way with the changing harmonic from the RB211 engines.

———

Chengdu, Central China

AIR FORCE MAJOR WANG FAN EASED BACK ON THE joystick of the final prototype Shenyang J-31 jet—designed exclusively for the People's Liberation Army Air Force. In response, China's newest fighter jet leapt upward like a catapult's missile from the PLAAF base in the flatlands surrounding the towering city of Chengdu.

It felt as he'd just been grasped by Chen Mei-Li. Never had a woman made him feel like such a man.

———

Get Drone *and fly into a whole series of action and danger!*
Available at fine retailers everywhere.
Drone

ABOUT THE AUTHOR

USA Today and Amazon #1 Bestseller M. L. "Matt" Buchman started writing on a flight south from Japan to ride his bicycle across the Australian Outback. Just part of a solo around-the-world trip that ultimately launched his writing career.

From the very beginning, his powerful female heroines insisted on putting character first, *then* a great adventure. He's since written over 60 action-adventure thrillers and military romantic suspense novels. And just for the fun of it: 100 short stories, and a fast-growing pile of read-by-author audiobooks.

Booklist says: "3X Top 10 of the Year." PW says: "Tom Clancy fans open to a strong female lead will clamor for more." His fans say: "I want more now...of everything." That his characters are even more insistent than his fans is a hoot.

As a 30-year project manager with a geophysics degree who has designed and built houses, flown and jumped out of planes, and solo-sailed a 50' ketch, he is awed by what is possible. More at: www. mlbuchman.com.

Other works by M. L. Buchman: (* - also in audio)

Action-Adventure Thrillers

Dead Chef
One Chef!
Two Chef!

Miranda Chase
*Drone**
*Thunderbolt**
*Condor**
*Ghostrider**
*Raider**
*Chinook**
*Havoc**
*White Top**

Romantic Suspense

Delta Force
*Target Engaged**
*Heart Strike**
*Wild Justice**
*Midnight Trust**

Firehawks
MAIN FLIGHT
Pure Heat
Full Blaze
*Hot Point**
*Flash of Fire**
Wild Fire
SMOKEJUMPERS
*Wildfire at Dawn**
*Wildfire at Larch Creek**
*Wildfire on the Skagit**

The Night Stalkers
MAIN FLIGHT
The Night Is Mine
I Own the Dawn
Wait Until Dark
Take Over at Midnight

Light Up the Night
Bring On the Dusk
By Break of Day
AND THE NAVY
Christmas at Steel Beach
Christmas at Peleliu Cove
WHITE HOUSE HOLIDAY
*Daniel's Christmas**
*Frank's Independence Day**
*Peter's Christmas**
*Zachary's Christmas**
*Roy's Independence Day**
*Damien's Christmas**
5E
Target of the Heart
Target Lock on Love
Target of Mine
Target of One's Own

Shadow Force: Psi
*At the Slightest Sound**
*At the Quietest Word**
*At the Merest Glance**
*At the Clearest Sensation**

White House Protection Force
*Off the Leash**
*On Your Mark**
*In the Weeds**

Contemporary Romance

Eagle Cove
Return to Eagle Cove
Recipe for Eagle Cove
Longing for Eagle Cove
Keepsake for Eagle Cove

Henderson's Ranch
*Nathan's Big Sky**
*Big Sky, Loyal Heart**
*Big Sky Dog Whisperer**

Other works by M. L. Buchman:

Contemporary Romance (cont)

Love Abroad
Heart of the Cotswolds: England
Path of Love: Cinque Terre, Italy

Where Dreams
Where Dreams are Born
Where Dreams Reside
Where Dreams Are of Christmas*
Where Dreams Unfold
Where Dreams Are Written

Science Fiction / Fantasy

Deities Anonymous
Cookbook from Hell: Reheated
Saviors 101

Single Titles
The Nara Reaction
Monk's Maze
the Me and Elsie Chronicles

Non-Fiction

Strategies for Success
Managing Your Inner Artist/Writer
Estate Planning for Authors*
Character Voice
Narrate and Record Your Own
Audiobook*

Short Story Series by M. L. Buchman:

Romantic Suspense

Delta Force
Th Delta Force Shooters
The Delta Force Warriors

Firehawks
The Firehawks Lookouts
The Firehawks Hotshots
The Firebirds

The Night Stalkers
The Night Stalkers 5D Stories
The Night Stalkers 5E Stories
The Night Stalkers CSAR
The Night Stalkers Wedding Stories

US Coast Guard

White House Protection Force

Contemporary Romance

Eagle Cove

Henderson's Ranch*

Where Dreams

Action-Adventure Thrillers

Dead Chef

Miranda Chase Origin Stories

Science Fiction / Fantasy

Deities Anonymous

Other
The Future Night Stalkers
Single Titles

SIGN UP FOR M. L. BUCHMAN'S NEWSLETTER TODAY

and receive:
Release News
Free Short Stories
a Free Book

Get your free book today. Do it now.
free-book.mlbuchman.com

Printed in Great Britain
by Amazon

55663559R00052